Daddy and the pink flash

written by Ellyn Bache   illustrated by Carol Tornatore

 Banks Channel Books
Wilmington, NC

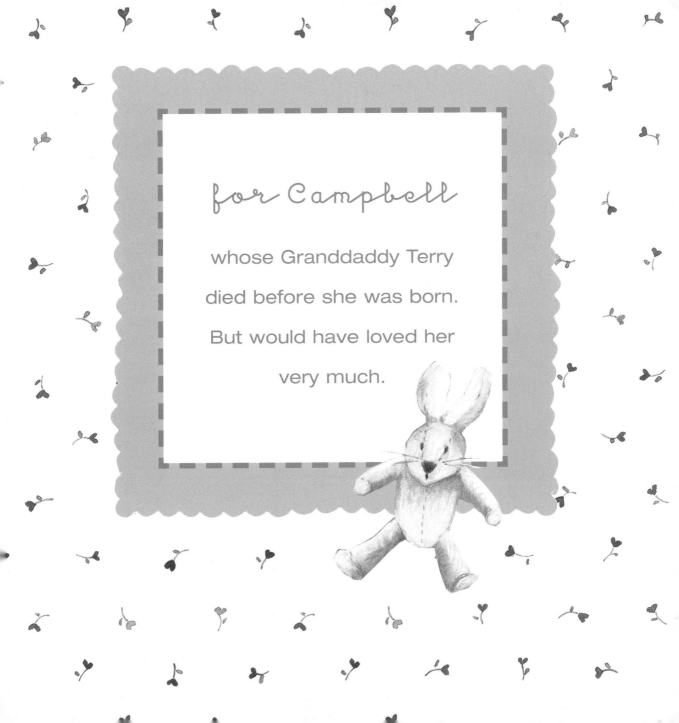

for Campbell

whose Granddaddy Terry
died before she was born.
But would have loved her
very much.

A long time ago

when Granddaddy Terry was a young man,
Aunt Beth was his first girl baby —

just like *you* are your dad's first little girl.

Beth

August 3
6 pounds/6 ounces
20 inches long

Now a lot of people, when they have their first baby, are sort of scared.

The baby is so little!

Why is she crying?

Is she hungry?

Is she wet?

What if Mommy and Daddy
do something wrong?

"You won't,"
said Great-Grandma Marian,
who had raised eight children
of her own.

She smiled at Beth —
who was even littler than you
when you were born —

"They grow up in spite of you,"
she told Granddaddy Terry.

"Enjoy her.

Have fun!"

So Granddaddy Terry did.

Lifting Beth high in the air
in her pink pajamas . . .

He-z-o-o

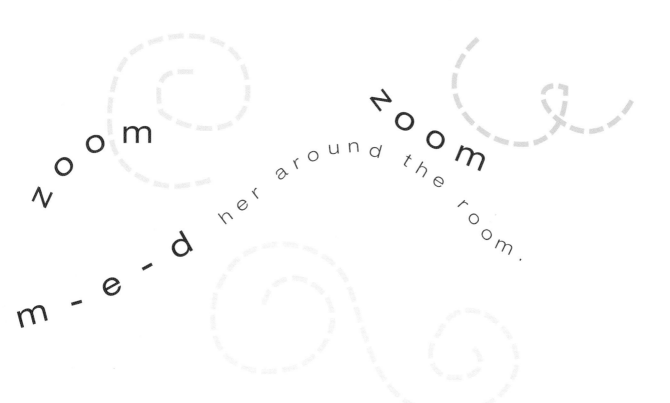

zoom zoom m-e-d her around the room.

"It's the *PINK FLASH!*"

he exclaimed as he twirled around and around.

Beth laughed.

"Yes, it's the Pink Flash!" Granddaddy Terry declared.
"Flying fearlessly around the room!
 She's the bravest baby in the world!"

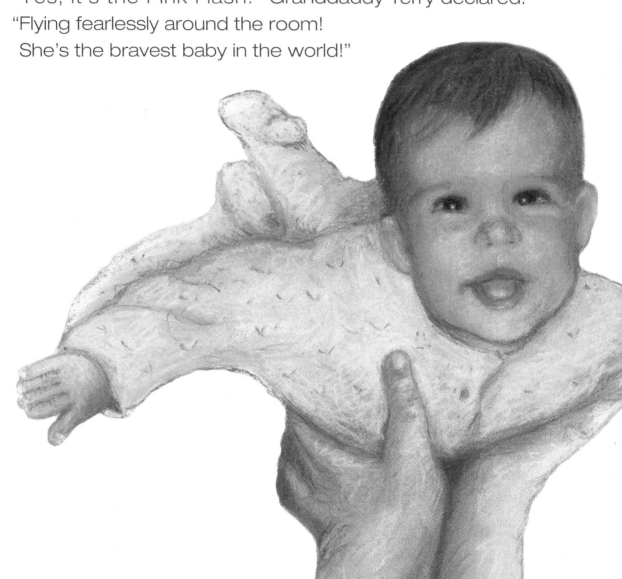

Yes!

Beth thought . . .
(though she was little and couldn't say so)

I am the Pink Flash!

The BRAVEST baby

in the world

Granddaddy Terry stood the Pink Flash on his lap.
She tried to push off with her feet.
She wanted to be back in the air!

"The Pink Flash loves to fly!" Granddaddy Terry shouted as he raised her toward the ceiling. She is the most athletic baby in the world!"

Yes! (the Pink Flash thought)

I am the most ATHLETIC baby in the world!

"Where's the kitty?" asked Granddaddy Terry.

The Pink Flash flew toward the couch
and reached out her hand to pet the kitty.

"Right!" said Granddaddy Terry.
"The Pink Flash is the smartest
baby in the world!"

The Pink Flash knew
he was right,

She was the
SMARTEST baby
in the world!

One day,

when she was older, the Pink Flash sat in
her high chair. She took a fistful of mashed
carrots and rubbed them on the tray.
She rubbed some mashed peas next to them.
They made a nice design.

"Look!" said Granddaddy Terry as he lifted
the Pink Flash so she could look down
at her creation.

"The Pink Flash is an artist!" "She's the most
artistic baby in the world!"

Yes! (the Pink Flash realized)

I am the most

Artistic

baby in the

world!

That was a long time ago.
Granddaddy Terry isn't around anymore.
Aunt Beth is all grown up now.

Mom, Dad and Beth

Kitty, Dad and Beth

Aunt Beth and Campbell

$\mathcal{B}$ut the Pink Flash

is still here . . .

YOU are the Pink Flash!

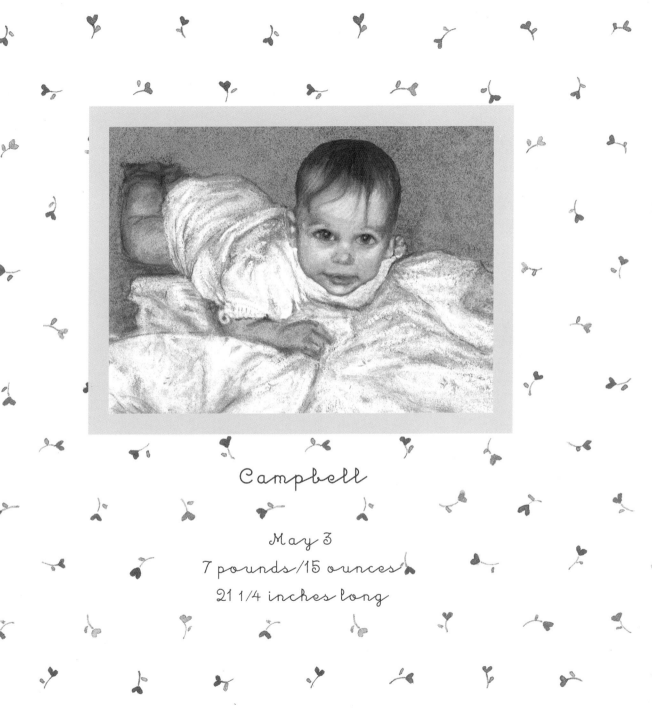

Campbell

May 3
7 pounds/15 ounces
21 1/4 inches long

Daddy helps you on take-offs and landings.

You fly around the room fearlessly.

Daddy shouts, "You are

the BRAVEST baby

in the world!"

You sit on Daddy's shoulders . . .

the most

ATHLETIC

baby in the world!

You find the kitty . . .

the SMARTEST baby

in the world!

Daddy says, "You make designs!"

the most

ARTISTIC

baby

in the world!

And dressed in all your pretty flying outfits,

the  most

STYLISH

baby

in the world, too!

Mommy, Daddy, and Campbell.